A Song for Lena

HILARY HORDER HIPPELY

illustrated by LESLIE BAKER

SIMON & SCHUSTER BOOKS FOR YOUNG READERS

SIMON & SCHUSTER BOOKS FOR YOUNG READERS
1230 Avenue of the Americas, New York, New York 10020

SIMON & SCHUSTER BOOKS FOR YOUNG READERS is a trademark of Simon & Schuster.
Printed and bound in Hong Kong by South China Printing Co. (1988) Ltd.
The text is set in Goudy Old Style. The illustrations are rendered in watercolor and pencil.
10 9 8 7 6 5 4 3 2 1 First Edition

Library of Congress Cataloging-in-Publication Data
Hippely, Hilary Horder.
A song for Lena / Hilary Horder Hippely ; illustrated by Leslie Baker. p.   cm.
Summary : Lena's grandmother tells about the time when her mother in Hungary shared
some freshly made strudel with a beggar who repaid her hospitality with a beautiful song.
Includes a recipe for apple strudel.
[1. Grandmothers—Fiction. 2. Hospitality—Fiction. 3. Apples—Fiction.
4. Cookery—Apples—Fiction. 5. Hungary—Fiction.] I. Baker, Leslie A., ill II. Title.
PZ7.H5977So   1996   95-44064   [E]—dc20   ISBN 0-689-80763-5

For my mother and father —H.H.H.

For Carolyn Croll—L.B.

When Lena's Grandma made strudel on the kitchen table she hummed a song from Hungary, soft and sweet and sad.

"Does the song have words?" Lena asked one day.

Grandma smiled. "No words, my Lenaka. Just feelings from the old country. When I sing I remember my mother in the courtyard, and my friend Anna, and the evening I first heard this song."

Lena tucked up her apron. "Where did the song come from?"

"That's a long story, Lena," said Grandma. "I'll tell it to you someday."

"Tell it to me now, Grandma," begged Lena. "I can sprinkle the flour while you talk."

Grandma laughed. "All right, then!"

You know when I was young I lived on a farm, Lena, a little farm sitting in a field of apple trees. When times were hard Papa had no money to pay for help, and at harvest he and Mama and my brothers and I picked apples from morning until night.

We were poor, but lots of people were poorer than we were. We always had food on the table, though sometimes at supper I was so tired I could hardly lift my spoon. Then Mama carried me to bed. "Times will get better," she whispered one night. "Tomorrow Anna's family comes to help sort apples. And when we're finished I'll make strudel on the kitchen table."

I sat up. "Can Anna and I help?"

"Of course." Mama smiled and tucked me in tight.

The next morning Anna's family arrived with the sun. Our fathers and brothers carried baskets up from the fields, and all day we sat in the courtyard sorting apples. The bruised ones were for cider. The good ones were for selling. And the little apples were for making strudel.

Anna and I wore checkered aprons, and Mama helped us push the rolling pin. She stretched and stretched the dough; then Anna and I covered it with butter and apples, and precious spoonfuls of sugar and raisins and nuts. Mama rolled the strudel into a crescent moon and slid it into the oven. "Now you girls can play," she told us. "We'll call you when it's time to eat!"

Anna and I flew down the hill. I remember the light that evening was so heavy and golden we could almost hold it in our hands. We sat on our favorite branch, just breathing in the sweet smell of baking floating down from the house.

Then suddenly Anna's eyes got big. "Shh!" she whispered.

I looked down. An old, tattered beggar man was coming along the road. He had a bag over one shoulder and a stick in one hand.

Papa said beggars slept in our fields at night, but I had never seen one so close. "Annaka!" I whispered. "What should we do?"

Anna put her finger on her lips and we kept as still as we could.

But the man stopped right under our tree. "Little girls," he called up to us. "I haven't eaten today. Could you run ask your mother for a piece of bread?"

Anna and I looked into the man's weary eyes. Then we climbed down and ran up to the house.

"There's a beggar man in the field!" we cried. "He's tired and wants some bread!"

Anna's father and mother and all our brothers were gathered around the table watching Mama take the strudel from the oven. Mama was smiling because it had turned out so nice—all crisp and golden brown.

For a moment nobody spoke.

"Bread?" Mama said at last, straightening up and pushing back her hair. "Beggars always ask for bread. I imagine once a year they can have strudel like the rest of us."

Then Mama cut a big slice of strudel and put it on a plate. She poured a mug of coffee from the pot. "You girls take this down to that poor soul," she said. "Let's see if it doesn't make him happy."

Anna carried the coffee and I carried the strudel. The man was leaning against our apple tree, dozing. "This is for you," I said, setting down the plate and mug. Then Anna and I ran back up to the house.

We were eating our own strudel when the strangest thing happened. A beautiful song came floating into the courtyard. I remember it seemed like that golden light was carrying it along, it was so soft and sweet and sad. We all just sat there, listening. Then my father got up and walked outside, and we followed.

The beggar man was standing in the field, playing a violin. I'll never forget that evening, Lena. We couldn't even move we felt so full of music, full of music and apple strudel. We listened for the longest time. Then after a while the light was gone, and the man disappeared down the road.

We never knew where he went. But somehow the man knew when it was strudel time, and he came back the next year. We brought him strudel and he played his violin song—that year and the year after.

Then one year he didn't come. The sky was dark and full of stars when Anna and I walked slowly back to the courtyard.

Papa pulled us close. "Now, now," he said. "Perhaps our friend isn't hungry anymore."

But I had begun to cry.

I felt Papa's arms around me. "You know, if we listen very closely," he said, "we might still hear the beautiful song."

"Could you hear it?" asked Lena.

"I heard the birds and the crickets," answered Grandma.

"And then I heard the song begin."

"Grandma," Lena whispered, "I can hear it too."

GRANDMA'S APPLE STRUDEL

(makes two strudels)

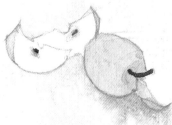

FILLING:

7 Granny Smith apples, peeled, cored & diced
1 1/4 cups golden raisins
1 cup brown sugar
juice of 1 lemon
2 tablespoons finely grated lemon rind
1 teaspoon cinnamon

DOUGH:

1 package phyllo dough,
   defrosted according to package directions
2 sticks melted butter
plain bread crumbs

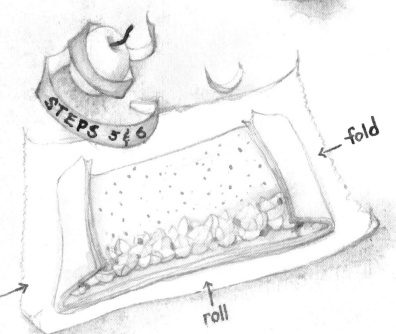

DIRECTIONS:

1. Preheat oven to 375°.

2. Toss all filling ingredients together. Set aside.

3. After defrosting the phyllo dough, carefully unroll the sheets on waxed paper. Immediately cover dough with another sheet of waxed paper, then a damp towel. Keep the phyllo dough covered until needed, as it dries out quickly and cracks.

4. To assemble a strudel, place one sheet of phyllo on a piece of waxed paper. Brush with some butter, making sure to include the edges. Sprinkle with approximately 1 tablespoon of bread crumbs. Place a second sheet of phyllo on top of the first. Brush with butter and sprinkle with crumbs. Repeat three more times until you've made five layers in all.

5. Spoon approximately one-half of the apple mixture along one long edge of the phyllo, leaving 1 1/2" empty on both ends. Fold the short sides in to enclose the filling. Brush the edges with butter.

6. Using the waxed paper, lift the long edge of dough with the filling and roll it over and over enclosing the apple mixture like a jelly roll. Place the strudel on a cookie sheet with the seam side down and brush all over with the butter.

7. Repeat steps 4 through 6 to make another strudel.

8. Bake 40-50 minutes until the strudel turns golden brown.

Enjoy!